Little Miss Muffet

Story by:
Lois Becker
Mark Stratton

Illustrated by:

Theresa Mazurek	Rivka
Douglas McCarthy	Fay Whitemountain
Allyn Conley-Gorniak	Su-Zan
Lorann Downer	Lisa Souza
Julie Armstrong	

This Book Belongs To:

Use this symbol to match book and cassette.

The nursery rhyme is called
"Little Miss Muffet."

Little Miss Muffet
Sat on a tuffet
Eating her curds and whey.
Along came a spider
And sat down beside her
And frightened Miss Muffet away.

Hector wanted to show Miss Muffet that she didn't need to be afraid of spiders. So he set off to find her.

Luckily, a hummingbird friend of Miss Muffet's just happened to be flying by and offered to show Hector the way to Miss Muffet's house.

Hector and the hummingbird arrived just as Miss Muffet was giving the hummingbirds their morning snack.

Then Miss Muffet took Hector into her playhouse. It was full of wonderful and mysterious things.

Hector and Miss Muffet were having a good time together. But all of a sudden she turned very pale and pointed to something on the wall.

It was just an old, dusty spiderweb.

Miss Muffet was so frightened that she ran out of the playhouse. And Hector waddled after her.

Miss Muffet soon forgot about the spiderweb because it was time for her midday snack of curds and whey. She and Hector took their bowls and sat on tuffets in the garden to eat.

No sooner had Miss Muffet put the spoon to her mouth than she saw a big, spidery shape on the wall behind her.

She was so scared, she dropped her bowl and ran to hide!

But Hector didn't move. He knew it was just a shadow. And sure enough, when he looked around, what should he see but a tiny spider, dangling from a thread and crying.

The spider told Hector that he was crying because he wanted to be friends with Miss Muffet and she wouldn't even look at him.

And then the spider did a wonderful thing. He plucked at his web as if he were playing a harp, and out came the most beautiful music.

"The Spider's Song"

I'm just a little spiderling
I'd never hurt a soul
But I fear that folks are scared of me.
Alas, alas, 'tis so!

But if you'd take a closer look
I'm sure that you would find
He's not the scary sort at all
The fear's all in your mind!

Let's get to know each other,
We might learn something new!
You could learn about me,
And I could learn about you!

So what if I only have eight legs?
And I have only two?
We can still explore together.
There's lots that we can do!

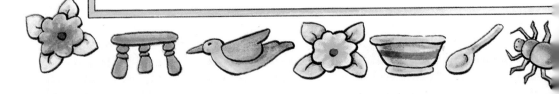

Oh, I could show you how I weave
These wondrous webs so fine,
And you could teach me all the little secrets,
Secrets of your kind!

Let's get to know each other,
We might learn something new!
You could learn about me,
And I could learn about you!

But if we're too afraid to look,
Then we will never see
All the magic all around us—
And the wonder that is me!

When Miss Muffet heard the spider's song, she crept out from her hiding place to get a better look at him.

Hector was glad that Miss Muffet wasn't scared of the spider anymore. But he warned her not to touch it.

Miss Muffet still thought spiderwebs were dirty.

But they're not always that way.

Of course, sometimes spiderwebs do get old and dusty, when nobody lives in them anymore.

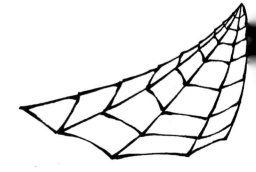

Just then, one of the hummingbirds came by.

It turned out that the hummingbird was building a nest.

When Hector and Miss Muffet saw the nest, they could hardly believe their eyes. It was made of spiderwebs!

The little spider wanted to see, too.

So he floated over on a silken thread he spun himself.

Miss Muffet was so impressed that she thought maybe they could be friends after all.

The only problem was, friends are supposed to call each other by their first names.

But Miss Muffet didn't like hers.

And the spider really didn't like his.

Luckily, Hector knew what to do.

"The Name Song"

Step right up!
Don't be shy!
Show a little pride!
It's not the name
That really counts,
It's what you've got inside!

So whether you're a Hector–
An Ignatius–
Or a Dan!
An Elmore–
Or a Heather!
An Ida–
Or an Ann!

A name is what you make it,
And this I know is true,
Folks will grow to like your name
Because of liking you!

Whether you're an Orville–
Or a Philbert–
Or a Ham!
An Ernestine–
A Zoe!
Naomi–
Or a Pam!

So step right up!
Don't be shy!
Show a little pride!
It's not the name
That really counts,
It's what you've got inside!

After Hector's song, they both felt much better. And the spider told Miss Muffet that he was Henry Aloysius Octavius Smalley the VIII.

But Miss Muffet called him Harry!

And Miss Muffet's first name turned out to be Patience.

But Harry called her Patty.

Now that Harry and Patty were friends,
Hector wanted to come home and tell me
all about the new things he had learned.
And that's exactly what he did!